THE FIVE CHINESE BROTHERS

THE

FIVE CHINESE BROTHERS

BY

CLAIRE HUCHET BISHOP

AND

KURT WIESE

Library of Congress Cataloging-in-Publication Data
Bishop, Claire Huchet. The five Chinese brothers.
Summary: Five brothers who look just alike outwit the
executioner by using their extraordinary individual qualities.
[1. Brothers–Fiction.   2. Individuality–Fiction]
I. Wiese, Kurt, 1887–   . II. Title.
PZ7.B5245Fi   1989   [E]   88-30740 (pbk.)
L.C. Number 38-27908 (hard.)
ISBN 0-698-20642-8 (paperback)
9   10   8
ISBN 0-698-20044-6 (hardcover)
53   55   57   59   60   58   56   54

To my father
who made me love China
and
To my mother
a born story-teller

THE FIVE CHINESE BROTHERS

ONCE upon a
time there were Five Chinese
Brothers and they all looked exactly alike.

They lived with their mother in a
little house not far from the sea.

The First Chinese Brother could swallow the sea. The Second Chinese Brother had an iron neck. The Third Chinese Brother could stretch and stretch and stretch his legs.

The Fourth Chinese Brother could not be burned.
And
The Fifth Chinese Brother could hold his breath indefinitely.

Every morning the First Chinese Brother would go fishing, and whatever the weather, he would come back to the village with beautiful and rare fish which he had caught and could sell at the market for a very good price.

One day, as he was leaving the market place, a little boy stopped him and asked him if he could go fishing with him.

"No, it could not be done," said the First Chinese Brother.

But the little boy begged and begged and finally the First Chinese Brother consented. "Under one condition," said he, "and that is that you shall obey me promptly."

"Yes, yes," the little boy promised.

Early next morning, the First Chinese Brother
and the little boy went down to the beach.
"Remember," said the First Chinese Brother,

"you must obey me promptly. When I make a sign for you to come back, you must come at once."
"Yes, yes," the little boy promised.

Then the First
Chinese Brother
swallowed the sea.

And all the fish were left high and dry at the bottom of the sea. And all the treasures of the sea lay uncovered.

The little boy was delighted. He ran here and there stuffing his pockets with strange pebbles, extraordinary shells and fantastic algae.

Near the shore the First Chinese Brother gathered some fish while he kept holding the sea in his mouth. Presently he grew tired. It is very hard to hold the sea. So he made a sign with his hand for the little boy to come back. The little boy saw him but paid no attention.

The First Chinese Brother made great movements with his arms and that meant "Come back!" But did the little boy care? Not a bit and he ran further away.

Then the First Chinese Brother felt the sea swelling inside him and he made desperate gestures to call the little boy back. But the little boy made faces at him and fled as fast as he could.

The First Chinese Brother held the sea until he thought he was going to burst. All of a sudden the sea forced its way out of his mouth, went back to its bed . . . and the little boy disappeared.

When the First Chinese Brother returned to the village, alone, he was arrested, put in prison, tried and condemned to have his head cut off.

On the morning of the execution he said to the judge:

"Your Honor, will you allow me to go and bid my mother good-bye?"

"It is only fair," said the judge.

So the First Chinese Brother went home . . . and the Second Chinese Brother came back in his place.

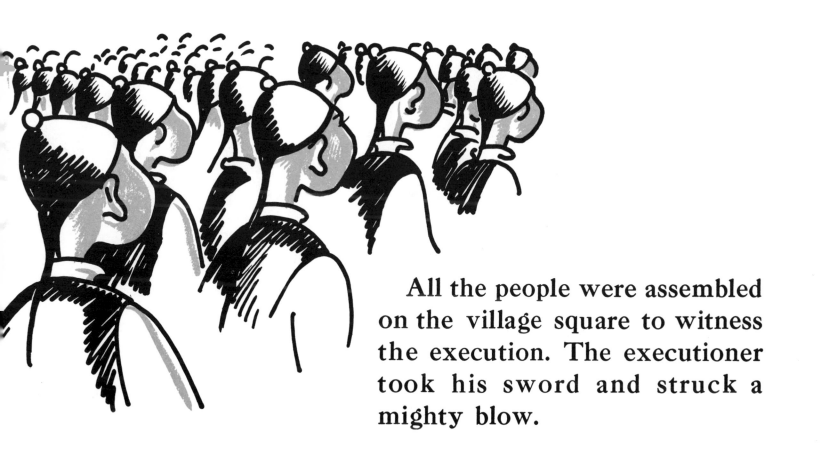

All the people were assembled on the village square to witness the execution. The executioner took his sword and struck a mighty blow.

But the Second Chinese Brother got up and smiled. He was the one with the iron neck and they simply could not cut his head off. Everybody was angry and they decided that he should be drowned.

On the morning of the execution, the Second Chinese Brother said to the judge:

"Your Honor, will you allow me to go and bid my mother good-bye?"

"It is only fair," said the judge.

So the Second Chinese Brother went home . . . and the Third Chinese Brother came back in his place.

He was pushed on a boat which made for the open sea.

When they were far out on the ocean,

the Third Chinese Brother was thrown overboard.

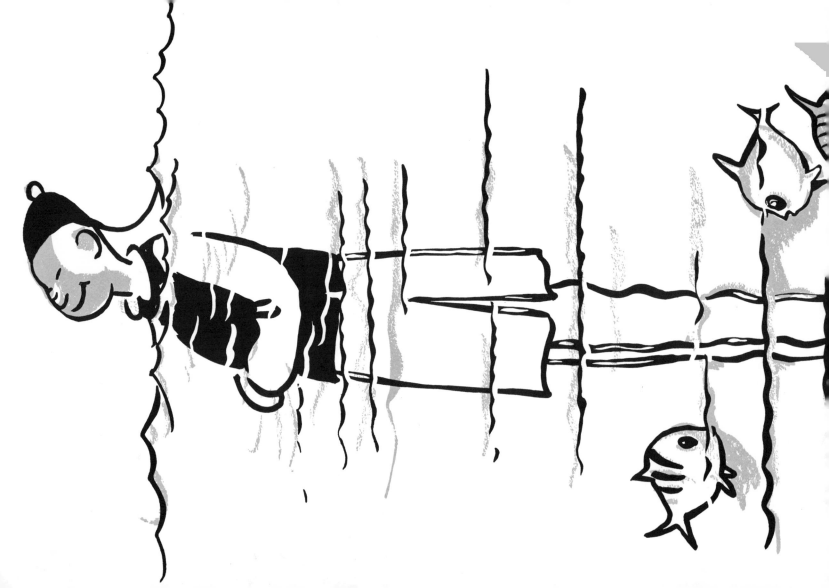

But he began to stretch and stretch and stretch his legs, way down to the bottom of the sea, and all the time

his smiling face was bobbing up and down on the crest of the waves. He simply could not be drowned.

Everybody was very angry, and they all decided that he should be burned.

On the morning of the execution, the Third Chinese Brother said to the judge:

"Your Honor, will you allow me to go and bid my mother good-bye?"

"It is only fair," said the judge.

So the Third Chinese Brother went home . . . and the Fourth Chinese Brother came back in his place.

He was tied up to a stake. Fire was set to it and all the people stood around watching it. In the midst of the flames they heard him say:

"This is quite pleasant."

"Bring some more wood!" the people cried.

The fire roared higher.

"Now it is quite comfortable," said the Fourth Chinese Brother, for he was the one who could not be burned. Everybody was getting more and more angry every minute and they all decided to smother him.

On the morning of the execution, the Fourth Chinese Brother said to the judge:

"Your Honor, will you allow me to go and bid my mother good-bye?"

"It is only fair," said the judge.

So the Fourth Chinese Brother went home . . . and the Fifth Chinese Brother came back in his place. A large brick oven had been built on the village square and it had been all stuffed with whipped cream. The Fifth Chinese Brother was shovelled into the oven, right in the middle of the cream, the door was shut tight, and everybody sat around and waited.

They were not going to be tricked again! So they stayed there all night and even a little after dawn, just to make sure.

Then they opened the door and pulled him out. And he shook himself and said, "My! That was a good sleep!"

Everybody stared open-mouthed and round-eyed. But the judge stepped forward and said, "We have tried to get rid of you in every possible way and somehow it cannot be done. It must be that you are innocent."

"Yes, yes," shouted all the people. So they let him go and he went home.

And
The Five Chinese
Brothers and their
mother all lived to-
gether happily for
many years.

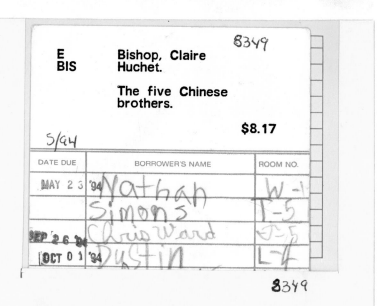

8349

8349

E	Bishop, Claire
BIS	Huchet.

The five Chinese
brothers.